The little hippo had spotted the pool of slurpy mud at the edge of the enclosure. He jumped right in, rolling around happily and splashing mud everywhere!

Look out for:

The Lonely Lion Cub

The Puzzled Penguin

The Playful Panda

The Silky Seal Pup

The Eager Elephant

The Pesky Polar Bear

The Lucky Snow Leopard

The Cuddly Koala

The Wild Wolf Pup

Amelia Cobb

Illustrated by **Sophy Williams**

With special thanks to Natalie Doherty

For Jack X

First published in the UK in 2016 by Nosy Crow Ltd
The Crow's Nest, 14 Baden Place, Crosby Row
London, SE1 1YW, UK

A CIP catalogue record for this book will be available from the British Library

5 7 9 10 8 6 4

Printed and bound in the UK by Clays Ltd, St Ives Plc

Papers used by Nosy Crow are made from wood grown in sustainable forests.

ISBN: 978 0 85763 602 7

www.nosycrow.com

Chapter One

Feathered Friends

Zoe Parker scooped up another handful of sunflower seeds and scattered them on the ground by her feet. They made a gentle pattering sound as they landed on the grass. "Breakfast time!" she called, and smiled as a flock of colourful birds fluttered down from the trees around her and began to peck eagerly at the seeds.

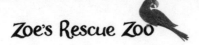

It was a sunny Saturday morning and Zoe was helping Alison, the bird keeper at the Rescue Zoo. They were in a huge enclosure, full of leafy trees and winding streams, where more than thirty different types of bird lived. Zoe and Alison had already given the hummingbirds, the toucans and the parakeets their breakfast. Now they had reached the lovebirds and the macaws, which were some of the brightest, prettiest birds at the zoo – and some of Zoe's favourites!

Meep was there too – although, Zoe thought with a grin, he wasn't really being that helpful. Meep was Zoe's best animal friend. He was a tiny grey mouse lemur, with soft fur, a long curly tail and big golden eyes. Meep also had a huge appetite,

and Zoe realised that he was eating some of the birds' breakfast as she and Alison were scattering the seeds on the ground. She giggled as he glanced around quickly to make sure that none of the birds were watching him, then snatched up a fat sunflower seed and started nibbling on it. *Cheeky little thing!* she thought to herself.

"You must be looking forward to the summer holidays!" said Alison, smiling at Zoe as she scattered handfuls of grain on to the grass. "Don't they start next week?"

Zoe nodded. "I can't wait!" she told Alison. "Six whole weeks off school. I can spend every day helping with the animals!"

Zoe wasn't just a visitor at the Rescue Zoo. She actually lived there! Zoe's great-uncle, Horace Higgins, was a famous

animal expert and explorer, who had decided to set up a zoo for any animals he met on his travels that were in need of a safe, friendly place to live. Zoe's mum, Lucy, was the zoo vet. Lucy and Zoe had moved into a little cottage at the edge of the zoo when Zoe was a baby, so she had grown up with animals all around her! Zoe loved animals more than anything, and wanted to be a vet herself one day. She knew how lucky she was to have such an amazing home.

"Zoe, I'm just going to pop to the store room and grab another bag of grain," explained Alison. "Back in a sec!"

"OK!" replied Zoe.

As Alison left the enclosure, Zoe heard a cross squawk behind her and turned to see what was going on.

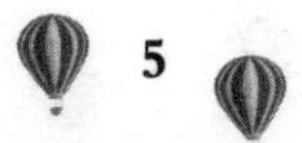

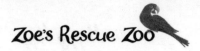

The mischievous little lemur was still helping himself to the birds' breakfast – and one of the birds, a bright-green lovebird named Cyril, had spotted what was going on! With a squeak, Meep grabbed one last seed and leaped quickly on to Zoe's shoulder just as Cyril swooped down towards him.

"Meep, you've already had your own breakfast back at the cottage," Zoe scolded her little friend gently. "These seeds and grains are for Cyril and his friends!"

"But I'm still a bit hungry, Zoe," explained Meep through a mouthful of food. "Besides, sunflower seeds are my favourite! As well as pumpkin seeds, bananas . . . oh, and blueberries, and peanuts. . ."

Zoe couldn't help giggling as Meep listed all the food he liked – which was a lot! "Well, no more now," she told him. "And say sorry to Cyril."

"Sorry, Cyril," grumbled Meep, and the lovebird fluttered his wings to show Meep that they were still friends.

Living at the Rescue Zoo wasn't the only unusual thing about Zoe. On her sixth birthday Zoe had found out that she had a special talent: she could talk to animals! But it was a secret, and nobody else knew – not even Zoe's mum or Great-Uncle Horace. Zoe was always careful never to speak to any of her animal friends when other people were around.

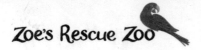

Just then, someone else opened the gate of the enclosure and stepped inside. "Hi, Mum!" called Zoe, waving. "Have you come to check Ruby?"

Lucy had the same dark, wavy hair as her daughter, but she usually wore it up in a ponytail, with a stethoscope around her neck. She had her special vet bag slung over one shoulder. "Hello, love," she called back. "Yes – I need to make sure her wing is healing properly."

Ruby was a scarlet macaw, with bright red, yellow and blue feathers. On a very windy day two weeks ago, a branch had snapped off a tree and fallen to the ground, catching the tip of Ruby's wing just before it landed. Lucy had been visiting every day to have a look at it.

Ruby was perching on a low branch this morning, and Lucy gently lifted the poorly wing and peered at it.

"Is it getting better?" asked Zoe anxiously.

Lucy nodded. "Luckily she didn't break the wing – that would have been much more serious. It's just bruised and sore. It looks like she's on the mend though. She'll be flying again in a week or two."

"Great!" said Zoe. She knew that Ruby was really missing being able to

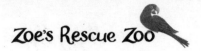

swoop around the huge enclosure with her friends. "Just in time for the summer holidays," she added. "I should be able to come and watch her every day!"

Lucy hesitated for a moment, before nodding again quickly. "Yes, you should," she replied, not meeting Zoe's eyes. "Now, I'd better get back to the zoo hospital – we're having a delivery of medicine this morning, so I need to check that everything we've ordered has arrived. I'll see you at home, OK, love?"

"OK," Zoe replied, but her mum was already rushing out of the enclosure, a worried expression on her face. Zoe frowned. "Meep, did you notice that?" she asked. "Mum was acting a bit strangely just then."

Meep looked puzzled too. "As soon as you mentioned the summer holidays she had a funny look on her face!" he chirped.

Zoe nodded. "The same thing happened last night," she remembered. "When I got home from school and we were having tea, I asked Mum what we were going to do over the holidays. I want to spend most of the time here at the zoo, but I was

hoping one day Mum might take me to the new water park that's just opened on the other side of town. But she changed the subject straight away!"

Ruby squawked reassuringly at Zoe, who smiled at the macaw. "You're right, she's probably just busy," Zoe replied. "But . . . well, she's always busy, and she never usually acts like this."

Cyril fluttered over to join them and chirped curiously, wanting to help. Zoe quickly explained the situation with her mum, and Cyril thought for a moment, then squawked eagerly.

"That's a good idea, Cyril – I'll just *ask* her what's wrong when we're back at the cottage later," said Zoe. "I'm sure it's nothing to worry ab—"

But both birds and Meep had turned

to look in the same direction, and Meep's sharp ears had pricked up. Zoe knew that meant the little lemur had heard something! Zoe listened carefully and heard a faint rumbling sound, getting louder and louder. "It might be the delivery van, coming to drop off the medicine Mum was talking about," she said.

But Meep was shaking his head. "I know what that sound is!" he squeaked. "It's the Rescue Zoo bus!"

Chapter Two
A Muddy Mess

Zoe's eyes lit up at Meep's words. "Then that means . . . Great-Uncle Horace is back!" she cried. "Quick, let's go and meet him, Meep. Bye, Ruby and Cyril – see you both soon!"

Zoe ran as fast as she could through the zoo, towards the main gates. It was still

early in the morning, so the zoo hadn't opened to visitors yet, and that meant the paths were empty. But the zoo was far from quiet! All the animals had heard the rumbling of the bus's engine and were barking, squeaking and trumpeting excitedly about Great-Uncle Horace arriving home.

"I can't wait to see him, Meep!" said Zoe breathlessly. "He hasn't been home for weeks!"

"And he might have brought a new animal with him!" Meep added excitedly.

"I hope so!" replied Zoe, grinning. Great-Uncle Horace spent most of his time exploring different parts of the world, looking for animals to help. When he came back to the Rescue Zoo, it was usually because he had found an animal

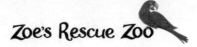

that needed a home. The last time, it had been a gorgeous little wolf pup named Shadow; before that, a baby koala called Kipp. Zoe really hoped Great-Uncle Horace had brought something back to the zoo this time!

Zoe and Meep rushed round a corner and arrived at the zoo gates just as a big yellow bus rumbled inside.

"You were right, Meep!" cried Zoe, pointing to the colourful hot-air balloon that was painted on the side of the bus.

This was the Rescue Zoo symbol. Sometimes Great-Uncle Horace travelled by motorbike or by helicopter, sometimes by bus or by the famous hot-air balloon itself – but whatever his mode of transport, it had the symbol painted on it somewhere!

As the bus rolled to a stop, Zoe heard footsteps and excited voices behind her. All the zookeepers had realised what was going on, and were rushing to meet Great-Uncle Horace, too! Lucy had also arrived, a huge smile on her face. Everyone gathered around the bus as a familiar figure leaped out.

Great-Uncle Horace had twinkling brown eyes and untidy white hair that stuck up at all angles. He had a battered safari hat on his head and wore a dusty safari jacket, with a compass hanging from a cord around his neck. On his shoulder perched a beautiful bird with deep-blue feathers. She was another macaw, like Ruby – but this one was very special. Kiki was a hyacinth macaw and had been Great-Uncle Horace's

companion ever since she was a tiny chick. Just like Zoe and Meep, Great-Uncle Horace and Kiki went everywhere together.

Great-Uncle Horace beamed as he looked around the crowd. "Hello, everyone!" he cried. "It's so good to be back! Now, where are my favourite niece and great-niece?"

"Here!" said Zoe, squeezing through the crowd and running up to Great-Uncle Horace. She jumped into his arms and he wrapped her up in a warm hug.

"Zoe, my dear! I've missed you so much," he told her. "And here's Lucy! I'm so happy to see you both. Kiki and I have travelled such a long way."

"We've really missed you!" Lucy told him, joining in the hug. "But where have

you come from this time?"

"And have you brought a new animal home with you?" added Zoe hopefully.

Great-Uncle Horace chuckled. "I certainly have!" he told Zoe. "I was exploring sub-Saharan Africa when I came across this little chap. I just know you're going to love him, Zoe."

Zoe and Meep exchanged an excited glance as Great-Uncle Horace called for some of the zookeepers to help lift a large wooden crate out of the back of the bus.

"What animals come from sub-Saharan Africa, Zoe?" squeaked Meep. "And what does 'sub-Saharan' mean anyway?"

"When I was looking up animals online the other day I saw those words, Meep. I think it means the part of Africa that's underneath the Sahara desert," Zoe

whispered back. "It's a really hot part of the world. And there are loads of different animals living there! Elephants, giraffes, rhinoceroses, lions, gazelles. . ."

"So the new animal could be anything!" chattered Meep, his eyes wide with excitement.

Zoe and Meep watched as the crate was lifted out of the bus and placed gently on the ground. There were lots of air holes drilled into it, and Zoe could hear a funny grunting sound coming from inside. Great-Uncle Horace unfastened the latch and opened up the crate. Everyone waited eagerly.

First a round, grey snout appeared, sniffing eagerly. Then a pair of bright black eyes followed, blinking in the sudden daylight. Finally, out of the crate

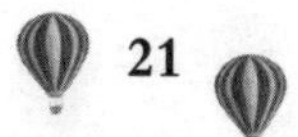

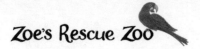

trotted a gorgeous baby hippo!

"Oh, wow! Great-Uncle Horace, he's so cute!" gasped Zoe, and on her shoulder Meep squealed in agreement.

The little hippo waddled straight up to Great-Uncle Horace and gave a friendly grunt. Then he stared round at the crowd of people, wagging his tiny tail excitedly. Zoe could tell he wasn't the least bit shy!

"He looks perfectly healthy and happy, Uncle Horace!" said Lucy, bending down to take a closer look at the hippo. "What happened to him?"

Zoe and Meep waited to hear the story. They both knew that Great-Uncle Horace only ever brought an animal back to the Rescue Zoo if it wasn't safe for them to stay in the wild.

"Kiki and I were travelling past a huge lake in a country called Tanzania," explained Great-Uncle Horace. "Suddenly I heard a frightened squeal, so I stopped the bus to take a look. I found this little chap stuck in some deep, sticky mud at the water's edge. I pulled him out and cleaned him up. And it was very lucky I did! That lake was full of crocodiles and he would have been in big

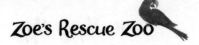

trouble if they'd heard his cries before I did."

"Oh dear," said Zoe, shuddering. "He must have been so frightened!"

Great-Uncle Horace nodded. "I did my best to find his family, but there were no other hippos to be seen for miles around, so I'm afraid he must have been an orphan," he said. "I knew I had to bring him straight back to the Rescue Zoo! Hippos have always been one of my favourite animals. Did you know, Zoe," he added eagerly, "that hippos are the third-biggest land animal in the world, after elephants and rhinos? They can grow to be absolutely enormous! And many people think that they are related to elephants and rhinos too – but actually their closest animal relatives are whales!"

"Really?" said Zoe, surprised. "Whales? But they live in the sea . . . hippos live on land!"

Great-Uncle Horace smiled. "Hippos do spend some of their time on land, especially when they are eating grass, but they'd much rather be in the water. Hippos love splashing around in lakes or ponds, and they are very good swimmers. They even give birth to their babies underwater!"

"Well, this little hippo is going to love our wonderful enclosure!" added another voice. Zoe smiled as Mo, the hippo keeper, stepped forward from the crowd. Mo looked after three hippos; Albert and Rona, and their daughter Hetty, who was two years old. Zoe thought about their home and realised Great-Uncle Horace

was right: the Rescue Zoo hippos spent almost all their time wallowing in their huge pond or their special mud bath.

"I think you're right, Mo. He'll love it. Let's take the little fellow there now!" said Great-Uncle Horace.

Great-Uncle Horace began to walk along the path towards the hippo enclosure, and the little hippo cheerfully trotted along beside him. Zoe could tell that he adored Great-Uncle Horace! She and Meep followed behind them with Lucy and Mo.

When they reached the hippo enclosure, Great-Uncle Horace smiled at Zoe and said, "Would you like to do the honours, my dear?"

Zoe knew what he meant straight away. She stepped up to the gate and

reached for the necklace around her neck. It was a simple chain with a pretty silver charm in the shape of a paw-print, and it had been a special present from Great-Uncle Horace. She lifted the charm and held it against a small panel on the gate, and with a quiet click it swung open. The necklace wasn't just a piece of jewellery – it was also a key, which opened every gate and door in the whole zoo!

Zoe stepped inside the enclosure and the little hippo rushed straight in after her, making lots of funny, excited grunting noises. The other hippos turned round to look at the new arrival, and as the baby hippo trotted up to them to say hello, Hetty gave a friendly, welcoming snort.

"He's going to settle in easily, I can tell!" chuckled Mo. "He's very confident."

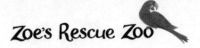

"I think he likes the mud bath," said Zoe. "Look!"

The little hippo had spotted the pool of slurpy mud at the edge of the enclosure and squealed eagerly. He raced straight up to it and jumped right in, rolling around happily and splashing mud everywhere!

"He definitely seems very happy in there!" laughed Lucy.

Suddenly there was an angry cry from the other side of the fence.

"Ugh, what a mess! There's mud all over the fence, all over the path – and all over *me*!"

"Oh no!" whispered Zoe to Meep as the gate flew open and a very cross, very muddy figure stood there, his hands on his hips and a scowl on his face. "It's Mr Pinch!"

Chapter Three
The Happy Hippo

"Just look at my uniform!" spluttered Mr Pinch angrily. "I'm covered in horrible mud!"

Mr Pinch was the Rescue Zoo manager. He was tall and skinny, and he was always in a bad mood. More than anything, he hated mess! His uniform was usually clean and tidy, and his zoo manager's hat and shoes polished and shiny. Now, though, he was covered in splodges of mud. "What is *that*?" he asked crossly, pointing to the little hippo, who was still happily rolling over and over in the gloopy mud bath.

"Oh, good morning, Mr Pinch! That's our newest addition to the Rescue Zoo," explained Great-Uncle Horace cheerfully. "As you can see, he loves his new home already. I'm sorry about your uniform but I'm sure the mud will come off."

"And I'll clean up the mess on the path," added Mo.

Mr Pinch frowned again at the little hippo and stomped off, muttering under his breath.

"I'll help you clean up, Mo," offered Zoe.

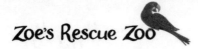

"That's very kind of you, Zoe," said Mo. "The hippos are always splashing mud on to the path, but usually I manage to clean up before Mr Pinch can see it. It was so unlucky that he walked past just then! I'll grab the hose from the store cupboard."

Lucy had to go and check on Gertie, a giraffe who was expecting a baby, and Great-Uncle Horace needed to go and unpack, so Zoe kissed them both goodbye and said she'd see them at home later. When they had left, Zoe whispered to Meep, "Now we can properly introduce ourselves to the little hippo!"

Zoe always tried to meet every new animal as early as possible after they arrived at the zoo, and explain that she could understand them. That way, if they were nervous or had any questions about their new home, they would know they could always ask Zoe for help. She just had to make sure she found the right moment to talk to them, when no one else was around!

Zoe walked over to the mud bath and crouched down next to it, with Meep perched on her shoulder. The little hippo sloshed happily straight through the mud towards them and grunted a friendly greeting. Where it wasn't covered in mud, his grey skin was very smooth and shiny, with pale-pink patches around his cheeks. Zoe thought his little ears looked like tiny shells or flower petals.

"Hi! My name's Zoe and this is my best friend Meep," Zoe began. "We live at the Rescue Zoo and we're excited that you've come to live with us! What's your name?"

The hippo's eyes lit up and he grunted eagerly. "It's lovely to meet you, Henry," Zoe said warmly. "What do you think of your new home?"

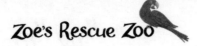

Henry answered by snorting happily and then rolling over again in the mud.

Zoe giggled. "I'm glad you like it so

much!" she replied with a laugh. "Albert, Rona and Hetty are all really friendly too. But I'm sorry about that grumpy man who was here before. That's Mr Pinch."

"He's always grumbling!" added Meep.

The hippo shook his little head and gave another cheerful grunt. Zoe was surprised that he didn't seem to mind at all. "Well, that's good, Henry. I'm glad he didn't upset you," she told him.

When Mo came back, carrying the end of a long hose to wash away the mud from the path outside the enclosure, Zoe said, "Can we call the new hippo Henry? I think it really suits him!"

"Henry the hippo. I like it!" replied Mo. "Gosh, he seems to be settling in very well, doesn't he? Usually it takes

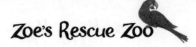

new animals a few days to get used to a new home, but Henry seems so happy already!"

Henry had wriggled out of the mud bath and was trotting around the enclosure, exploring and exchanging friendly grunts with the other hippos. While Mo hosed away the mud, Zoe fetched the *Wet Floor* sign to warn visitors that the path underfoot might be slippery. She found herself humming a cheerful tune and realised she was feeling happy too. The little hippo's good mood seemed to have rubbed off on her!

When they were done, Mo fetched a crate of chopped-up fruit and vegetables, and Zoe helped him feed the hippos. Henry especially liked the juicy chunks of melon, gobbling them up hungrily.

"That's reminded me – I should go home for my own lunch!" said Zoe, feeling her tummy rumble. "Can I come back and see Henry again tomorrow, Mo?"

"Of course, Zoe. Come any time you like," Mo told her, smiling.

When Zoe got home there was a delicious smell drifting from the kitchen. "Mum, are we having sausages for lunch?" Zoe called hopefully. Sausages and mash was one of Zoe's all-time favourite meals!

Lucy popped her head round the kitchen door. "Yes, we are! It will be ready in fifteen minutes, so go and get changed out of those muddy things. And make sure you wash your hands really well if you've

been playing with the baby hippo."

"We're naming him Henry," Zoe explained as she went to get changed. "He's so cute, Mum. And he seems really happy here already!"

A few minutes later Zoe was all cleaned up and ready to eat. As she and her mum ate, Zoe remembered the birds' advice from this morning, and decided to try asking about the summer holidays again.

"Mum," she began, "do you think, one day in the holidays, we could go to the big outdoor adventure playground that we've driven past a few times? I think it looks brilliant – it's got a huge tyre swing and a trampoline! And I think it's free to go there," she added, suddenly wondering if her mum hadn't seemed very keen on going to the new water park because the

tickets cost a lot of money.

Lucy didn't say anything for a moment, and Zoe watched as she pushed her food around her plate, a slight frown on her face. Zoe wasn't sure what she'd done wrong. Usually she and her mum loved chatting about all the fun things they'd be able to do in the school holidays. Of course, they both loved spending time at the zoo more than anything, and Lucy couldn't leave the animals for very long, so they didn't often travel abroad. But every year they went on day trips to water parks and museums, and sometimes to the seaside. Zoe could tell there was something bothering her mum, though she couldn't imagine what it might be.

Lucy put her knife and fork down, took a deep breath and turned to Zoe

with a cautious smile. "Listen, love. There's something I've been meaning to—"

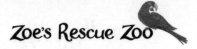

"*Briiing! Briiing!*"

Right then the telephone rang, cutting Lucy off in the middle of her sentence. She stood up and went into the hall to answer it.

"Meep, what's going on?" Zoe

whispered. "I think Mum was going to tell me something then, and it seemed like it was serious."

Meep, who was nibbling a banana for his own lunch, shook his head. "I don't know!" he chirped. "Maybe she'll explain when she comes back to the table?"

But when Lucy put the phone down and came back into the kitchen, she didn't sit down again, but grabbed her jacket and her vet bag. "That was Frankie, the giraffe keeper," she explained. "Gertie the giraffe is about to have her baby! I need to rush over there straight away, to help with the delivery. These things can take hours, so Great-Uncle Horace is going to come over and spend the rest of the day here, in case I'm not back until late."

Zoe nodded. She was excited about the baby giraffe – Zoe loved helping out with the newborn animals at the zoo. But she was also a bit disappointed that her mum hadn't been able to finish telling her whatever she'd been about to say. "Hopefully we'll find out tomorrow!" she whispered to Meep.

The doorbell rang shortly afterwards. When Zoe ran to open the door, Great-Uncle Horace was standing there with Kiki perched on one shoulder, holding up an ice-cream cone in each hand. "I stopped at the zoo café on the way over here. I thought we could have a treat, as it's a sunny day!" he announced. "Now, would you like chocolate or strawberry?"

"Chocolate, please!" answered Zoe, grinning.

Lucy left for the giraffe enclosure straight away, promising to ring as soon as there was any news about the baby, and Great-Uncle Horace and Zoe sat on a bench in the little cottage garden, eating their ice creams. After a few bites, Zoe decided to tell Great-Uncle Horace what she was worrying about. Although he could be very forgetful at times, he was also the wisest person Zoe knew. She could always talk to him if she had a problem.

"Great-Uncle Horace, do you know

if Mum is OK?" she asked. "She's been acting quite strangely over the last few days, and I don't know why."

Great-Uncle Horace paused for a moment before answering. "I'm sure it's nothing to worry about, my dear. Perhaps she had her mind on the baby giraffe, or one of the poorly animals she's treating at the moment." He was trying to reassure her, but Zoe thought *he* was sounding a bit strange now, too! "I hear the new hippo is settling in well!" he added, changing the subject. "Mo tells me you've named him Henry. He's a cheerful little fellow, isn't he?"

Zoe nodded. "He's great," she said. "I love it when you bring new animals home, Great-Uncle Horace. What do you think you'll bring with you next?"

"Well, the next place I plan to visit is the Arctic," explained Great-Uncle Horace. "Actually, I'll have to set off next week. There's a special six-week project at an animal research centre there, and I've been asked to go and help. So I won't be able to stay at the Rescue Zoo for very long this time, I'm afraid."

"Next week?" said Zoe, her heart sinking. Both Mum and Great-Uncle Horace were acting strangely *and* he was going away again so soon. Zoe's happy mood from earlier in the day was disappearing fast!

Chapter Four
A Curious Conversation

Great-Uncle Horace smiled at Zoe. "Cheer up, my dear," he said. "I know what will put a smile back on your face. I think Mo will be giving the hippos another feed in a little while. Shall we go and visit them?"

"Yes, please!" said Zoe. Great-Uncle

Horace was right – the idea of visiting the hippos had her feeling better already. It was hard to feel down when there was a gorgeous baby animal to play with!

The paths were still busy as Zoe and Great-Uncle Horace walked through the zoo, and lots of the visitors were enjoying ice creams or cold drinks. Zoe smiled as they passed the lions and saw Leonard and Rory sprawled out on the grass, basking in the sun.

When they arrived at the hippo enclosure, Zoe couldn't help chuckling. The path outside, which had been spotlessly clean when she'd left earlier that day, was once again covered in muddy splashes and puddles. "I think Henry *really* likes playing in the mud bath," she told Great-Uncle Horace. "But poor Mo

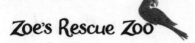

is going to end up spending all his time cleaning!"

Inside the enclosure, Albert and Rona were wallowing in the deep pool, staying nice and cool in the afternoon sunshine, while Hetty and Henry chased each other round the outside of the mud bath, grunting happily. Mo waved when he saw Zoe and Great-Uncle Horace step inside the enclosure. Zoe thought he looked a little tired!

"Henry's getting along brilliantly with all the other hippos, especially Hetty," Mo told them, rubbing his forehead with a weary smile. "But four hippos together is a lot of hard work! They've made quite a bit of mess. Mr Pinch came along earlier to check that the path had been cleaned properly, and just as he arrived Henry jumped in the mud and splashed him again! Mr Pinch was really cross. He's complained twice about all the noise they've been making, too."

The enclosure was muddier, messier and noisier than Zoe had ever seen it before. But little Henry was so sweet and funny that it was hard to mind. They all watched and laughed as he ran excitedly around them, hid from Hetty behind tree trunks and rocks, and jumped playfully into muddy puddles, squeaking and grunting eagerly.

Suddenly Great-Uncle Horace's walkie-talkie crackled and Zoe heard her mum's voice. "Come in, Uncle Horace! I just wanted to share the good news: Gertie's baby has just arrived safely! It's a male, and he's gorgeous!"

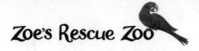

"Come in, Lucy! This is Uncle Horace. That's wonderful news!" exclaimed Great-Uncle Horace, holding up his own walkie-talkie. "How is Gertie?"

The walkie-talkie crackled again. "She's fine!" replied Lucy. "She and the calf are sleeping now I'll be coming home soon. How is Zoe? She seemed a little down when I left. I was just about to tell her about—"

Great-Uncle Horace quickly interrupted her. "Zoe's standing right here next to me, as a matter of fact! We're at the hippo enclosure, visiting cheeky young Henry." He smiled at Zoe, then took a few steps away and spoke again into the walkie-talkie, though in a hushed voice this time. Zoe couldn't hear what he and her mum were talking about any more, but now she felt sure that they were keeping something from her. And she was becoming more and more curious to find out what!

A couple of days later, Zoe was walking home from school with her friends Jack and Nicola. Lucy was busy at the zoo, looking after the newborn giraffe, so Nicola's mum had offered to see Zoe

home. Nicola was counting down the days until the summer holidays started.

"We're going camping in France for two weeks!" she said excitedly. "And we're setting off as soon as school finishes on Friday, so we can catch the ferry on Friday night! Mum and Dad practised putting our tent up in the back garden yesterday. I've even got my own little area to put my sleeping bag in. It's going to be really cosy!"

"We're not going away but my auntie and my cousins are coming to visit us from America!" said Jack, sounding thrilled. "We're going to take them to that new adventure playground, the one with the massive tyre swing and the giant trampoline!"

"Oh, I'd love to go there!" said Zoe.

"I asked my mum if she'd take me, but she's being a bit strange about the holidays. I don't think we're going to do anything special."

"But you already live in the best place in the whole world!" pointed out Nicola, and Jack nodded. "If I lived at the Rescue Zoo I'd never want to go anywhere else. I'd jump out of bed as soon as I woke up, eat my breakfast as quickly as I could, run out of the house and spend all day with the animals!"

"That *is* what I do!" said Zoe, grinning. "You're right – I don't really need to go anywhere else in the holidays. Even if I stayed at the zoo for the entire six weeks, I'd be happy."

When they reached the Rescue Zoo and Zoe waved goodbye to her friends,

she was still feeling cheerful. Meep was waiting for her in his usual spot at the zoo gates, and she smiled as he jumped up on to her shoulder. "Let's go straight to the hippo enclosure and visit Henry," she told him.

The zoo paths were busy with visitors that afternoon, and there was an especially big crowd gathered outside the hippo enclosure, where Mo had fixed a sign saying: *We have a new member of the hippo family, all the way from Tanzania: please welcome Henry to the Rescue Zoo!*

"I loved seeing that gorgeous hippo!" Zoe heard a girl with long red hair telling her little sister. "I wish we could take him home with us."

Zoe slipped through the crowd and let herself and Meep into the enclosure using her special necklace, making sure the gate was safely closed behind them. She heard the girls gasp, and the younger sister whispered, "Look, that girl is allowed to go inside! She must be a bit like a zoo keeper. She's *so* lucky!"

Zoe smiled. Just like her friends had said, she really was lucky!

Rona and Albert were snoozing in the sunshine, but Henry and Hetty were awake and playing in the deep pool in the centre of the enclosure. Zoe walked over to the pool and watched them,

giggling. Hetty was showing Henry that she could dive right to the bottom of the water, touching the rocks below with her snout, before surfacing again. Henry was squealing and snorting excitedly, and trying to copy the older hippo, paddling his wrinkled little legs as hard as he could. Even though he was very young and small, Henry was still an excellent swimmer.

Zoe crouched down next to the pool and both hippos paddled towards her. "You look like you're having a lot of fun!" Zoe said, smiling. "I've got an idea! Wait there."

She ran to the little store cupboard at the edge of the enclosure, where Mo kept all his equipment. Inside was a bright-green bouncy ball. Zoe took it back to

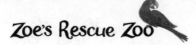

the pond and held it up. "I'll throw the ball into the water," she said. "The first hippo to reach it wins a point!"

Henry and Hetty grunted eagerly as Zoe threw the ball in. Hetty got to it the first time, but Henry was very quick and managed to dart through the water and nudge it with his snout the second time.

"That's a point each so far!" Zoe told them with a laugh – but she stopped talking quickly when Meep gave a warning squeak. Someone was coming!

"Ah, there you are, Zoe!" said a voice behind her.

Zoe turned to see Great-Uncle Horace stepping inside the enclosure. He was

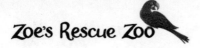

laden with several bags and a suitcase. "I had a feeling I might find you here. I've come to say goodbye, my dear."

Zoe put the bouncy ball on the ground, feeling her heart sink. "Are you leaving right now?" she asked.

Great Uncle Horace nodded. "I'm afraid so. I have to catch a plane to the Arctic research project this evening. I've packed all my warmest clothes, because it's going to be very cold when I get there! And plenty of my favourite custard cream biscuits," he added. "I'm not sure I'll be able to buy them in the Arctic, so I put as many packets in my suitcase as I could."

Zoe smiled as she imagined Great-Uncle Horace's battered old case stuffed with woolly jumpers and packets of biscuits. "I'm really going to miss you!" she told him.

Great-Uncle Horace held his arms out and Zoe ran into them for a hug. "I'll miss you too, Zoe," he told her. "But I'll send you lots of postcards, and I'll be home in six weeks."

Six weeks is ages, Zoe thought sadly. But she managed a brave nod, and waved as he walked back down the path, Kiki perched on his shoulder. As Great-Uncle Horace turned the corner and disappeared out of sight, she sighed,

and Meep jumped into her arms for a cuddle. "Let's keep playing the ball game with Hetty and Henry," the little lemur suggested. "It might cheer you up!"

"Good idea, Meep," replied Zoe, and threw the ball for a third time to the excited hippos. But her heart wasn't in it any more – especially when she heard a loud, grumpy voice coming from the other side of the fence.

"Excuse me, excuse me! Zoo manager coming through!" Mr Pinch snapped, pushing through the crowd of visitors and marching into the hippo enclosure. He frowned when he saw Zoe. "I should have known you'd be here again, Miss Parker!" he told her. "Encouraging the hippos to make even more mess, I'll bet!" he added, nodding at the ball.

"We're just playing, Mr Pinch," Zoe told him, doing her best to be polite.

"That's the whole problem!" Mr Pinch snapped. "Ever since that new one arrived, these hippos have done nothing but play and swim and splash and roll around in the mud! It's causing absolute chaos! Every time I walk past there are nasty, muddy puddles on the path outside. It's a health and safety nightmare. What if one of our customers slipped and fell? Three hippos were bad enough, but four is just *too* many."

Zoe stared at him, her heart sinking. Just then she saw her mum appear at the entrance to the enclosure.

"Is everything all right, Mr Pinch?" Lucy asked.

Mr Pinch shook his head crossly. "No,

everything is not all right! This enclosure is a disgrace. It is far too muddy and messy and noisy, and dangerous too! Those hippos had better start behaving themselves because I will not allow this in my zoo!" Mr Pinch scowled and stomped off down the path.

"Oh dear," said Lucy, looking around. "It *is* looking a bit crowded and messy in here. Maybe Mo needs a little bit more help from some of the other zoo keepers."

Zoe bit her lip and glanced at Hetty and Henry, who were still splashing around in their pool. *I need to warn the hippos to try and play a bit more carefully*, she thought. *Who knows what Mr Pinch might do if they keep making such a mess?* But she knew she couldn't risk speaking to them with her mum right there. "Mum, is it

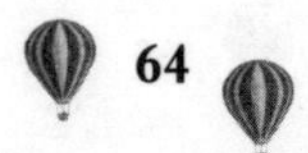

OK if I stay here with the hippos for a bit longer before I come home for tea?" she asked, but Lucy shook her head.

"That's why I've come to find you, Zoe. I need to have a talk with you about something, back at home." She was looking rather serious.

"What's going on, Zoe?" Meep hissed in Zoe's ear.

Zoe shook her head, but she thought she had an idea. Maybe her mum was finally going to explain why she had been acting so strangely!

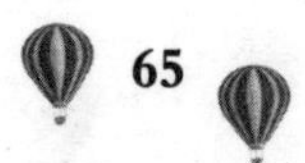

Chapter Five
Lucy's News

The zoo was still bustling with visitors as they walked back to the cottage. Zoe sighed a bit as she walked along the path with Lucy. She was missing Great-Uncle Horace already!

"At least we'll still be here for the summer, even if Great-Uncle Horace

won't be," Zoe said to her mum – but as she did, Zoe thought she saw an anxious expression cross her mum's face. She was *really* curious now, and had a nervous, wobbly feeling in her tummy. What was her mum going to tell her?

Back at the cottage, Lucy hung her vet's bag on the hook by the front door and went to sit at the kitchen table. She patted the chair next to her. "Come and sit down, love. I need to tell you something."

Zoe slid into her seat and Meep perched on her shoulder, just as curious as Zoe. Lucy took a deep breath. "I'm sorry I've been a bit distracted lately, Zoe," she said. "I've had to make quite a hard decision over the last week, and I've been feeling a bit worried about telling you. You see . . . Great-Uncle Horace isn't the only person

who was invited to go on the Arctic research trip. I was asked to go too."

Zoe's eyes opened wide. "Really? Wow!" This wasn't what she'd been expecting at all! Surely this was good news?

"One of the biggest parts of the trip is researching polar bears," Lucy explained. "When I was studying to become a vet, I had a special interest in them. I learned a lot about them from one of my teachers. That's one of the reasons we have such a wonderful polar bear enclosure here at the Rescue Zoo."

Zoe nodded. Her mum loved all kinds of animals, but Zoe knew that polar bears were one of her mum's special favourites.

"My old teacher is the person who is in charge of this expedition," Lucy went on. "She's also a very good friend of Great-

Uncle Horace, and she asked us both to join the trip."

"Wow, Mum – that's brilliant!" said Zoe. "But . . . Great-Uncle Horace has already set off. Does that mean you decided not to go with him?"

Lucy shook her head. "Great-Uncle Horace knew straight away that he wanted to join the project but it's taken me a little bit longer to decide," she told Zoe.

"So what are we going to do?" asked Zoe. She didn't understand why her mum had been so worried about telling her this news. It sounded so exciting! What an adventure. "Please tell me you said yes! Would we set off straight away, or would we wait for me to finish the school term?"

"Well, that's the problem, love," Lucy

said gently. "There are no children allowed on the trip. Great-Uncle Horace and I explained to my old teacher just how fantastic you are around animals, but I'm afraid it's just the rules."

"Oh," said Zoe, feeling disappointed. She was so used to being allowed to spend just as much time with all the animals as the grown-up keepers at the zoo, it was strange to be told that something was for adults only. "Well, that's all right. I'll just look after the animals here at the zoo until you get back."

Lucy shook her head. "I'm sorry, Zoe, but I can't leave you here on your own," she explained. "With both me and Great-Uncle Horace away, there'll be no one to look after you. So . . . I've asked your Auntie Edna if you can go and stay with

her while we're away."

Zoe stared at her mum, disappointment turning to horror. "Auntie Edna?" she repeated, hoping she might have

misheard. "But . . . I don't know her at all. And she lives really far away from the Rescue Zoo, so I wouldn't even be able to come home and visit. And. . ." Zoe suddenly remembered the very worst thing about Auntie Edna.

"And she's allergic to animals," finished

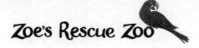

Lucy, nodding. "I know, love. I'm really sorry. It means that Meep will have to stay here at the zoo, I'm afraid. He'll be really well looked after with the lemurs and monkeys over the summer though."

Zoe felt Meep start to skitter back and forth between her shoulders anxiously. She knew immediately what her tiny friend would be thinking. "But Meep doesn't *like* living in an enclosure, even the lovely big one that the other lemurs are in," she said, feeling desperate. "That's why he came to live with us in the first place." Meep had come to the Rescue Zoo when he was a little baby, and he'd never liked being kept in any kind of enclosed space.

Lucy sighed. "I knew this wouldn't be what you wanted to hear, Zoe," she said.

"That's why I was so worried about telling you. But going on this trip is really important to me, love. I've always dreamed about going to the Arctic, but I've never had the chance before and I might never have it again. I'll learn so much, especially about polar animals, so I'll be an even better vet when I get back."

Zoe looked at her mum's hopeful face and knew what she had to say – even though it was really hard. "I understand, Mum," she said, nodding and trying her best to smile. "I was just . . . a bit surprised. But I really don't mind. You should definitely go. It will be brilliant. Besides, maybe Auntie Edna will turn out to be really fun." As Zoe said this, a picture swam into her mind: a thin lady

with grey hair and a scowl on her face, snapping at Zoe not to stroke a cat on the pavement outside in case she brought any hairs inside the house. She shivered.

Lucy reached over and hugged Zoe. "Thank you, Zoe. I was so nervous about telling you but you're being so grown up about this. I know you understand how much this means to me. And I promise that next summer we'll do something to make up for it – we'll go on a proper holiday, somewhere lovely and hot by the seaside, with lots of other children for you to make friends with."

But Zoe didn't mind about going on holiday. She just wanted to stay at home for the summer with all her animal friends – and with her best friend, Meep, most of all.

After tea, when Zoe had brushed her teeth and put on her pyjamas, she and Meep got into bed and cuddled each other tight.

"I don't want to be away from you for six whole weeks, Meep!" Zoe whispered, feeling a big sad lump in her throat.

"Me neither," squeaked Meep miserably, rubbing his furry little face against Zoe's neck. "This is going to be the worst summer ever!"

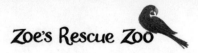

Zoe didn't get very much sleep that night. When she woke up the next morning she felt tired and cross, and she wasn't looking forward to school. Today was the last day of term, and she knew her friends would be chatting excitedly about all the fun things they had planned for the holidays.

Lucy had left for the zoo hospital early, so that she could use the computer there to book her flight to the Arctic. She had left a plate of toast and a pot of raspberry jam on the kitchen table for Zoe's breakfast, along with a cheery note wishing Zoe a fun last day at school. Zoe managed a few mouthfuls of toast but she didn't feel very hungry.

Meep was feeling glum too. "I don't think I can eat my breakfast today," he told Zoe very seriously. "I'm too sad."

Zoe couldn't help smiling. "Meep, you're never too sad to eat breakfast," she told him. "What about one little banana?"

"Well . . . maybe I could manage just one," Meep agreed.

Suddenly Zoe had an idea. "Meep, let's go and visit Henry before I go to school." She picked up her school bag. "If anyone can cheer us both up, it's him! He's always happy."

They walked through the zoo, passing zookeepers on the path on their way to give different animals their breakfasts. Zoe smiled and said hello, but she didn't feel like stopping to chat to anyone.

When Zoe and Meep arrived at the hippo enclosure and opened the gate to walk inside, Henry trotted straight

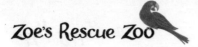

over to meet them. He looked up at Zoe curiously, nudged her foot with his little head and gave a grunt.

"How did you know that something was wrong, Henry?" Zoe replied, smiling. She crouched down and stroked his head. "You're right – I am feeling sad about something." She sighed. "I found out last night that I've got to leave the Rescue Zoo for the summer, and stay with a great-auntie who I barely know. I'm going to miss everyone here so much."

Henry rubbed his head against Zoe's leg again and gave a cheerful snort. Zoe smiled. "That's true, Henry," she replied. "We'll just have to have even more fun than usual before I leave, so that I've got lots of fun memories to think about while I'm away!"

Henry gave another little grunt, his eyes bright. Then he turned and rushed away from them, squealing eagerly at the other hippos, who were all wallowing happily in their mud bath. Zoe and Meep glanced at each other. "Henry wants us to play chase with the hippos," Zoe said

doubtfully. "I'm not sure if that's a good idea, Meep. Henry's still quite little, but the others are really big and heavy, and Great-Uncle Horace says that hippos can run really fast. I think we'd better leave them to it!"

"Yes, I don't want to get squished!" chirped Meep, shaking his little head.

Zoe smiled, and then she and Meep watched as the other hippos grunted excitedly back at Henry, then stomped out of the mud and started to chase after him. Henry grunted instructions for his game, saying he had to run once around the whole enclosure and then get back to the mud bath without any of them catching him. The little hippo ducked underneath low branches and squeezed through narrow gaps between rocks that

the bigger hippos couldn't manage, so at first he got a head start. Then, as he trotted back towards the mud bath, the others started to catch up with him.

"Oh dear, Meep," Zoe said anxiously. "The mud bath is right next to the fence – and all the hippos are running straight towards it. I don't know if they're going to be able to stop in time!"

Zoe and Meep held their breath as Henry leaped into the mud bath, squealing happily. A moment later Albert, Rona and Hetty thundered after him. But Albert and Rona were charging so fast that they couldn't slow down. Their tough grey feet slid through the slurpy mud, and they smashed straight into the fence next to it – and right through it! They landed on a stretch of empty grassland on the

other side of the fence, and both looked around in surprise.

"Oh no!" cried Zoe. "Meep, they've broken through the fence!"

She rushed over to see how much damage the playful hippos had done.

Pieces of wood lay scattered all over the grass, and there were huge puddles of

gloopy mud everywhere. Henry leaped out of the mud bath and trotted through the gap curiously after Albert, Rona and Hetty, making cheerful little snorting noises. He immediately started exploring this new area of the zoo excitedly.

Zoe heard footsteps and turned to see Mo running down the path, a look of horror on his face as he saw what had happened.

"I can't believe it!" he gasped. "Quick, Zoe – we'd better get the hippos back in their enclosure and try to clean this mess up before Mr Pinch sees. He's on his morning walk around the zoo now, so he'll be coming this way any moment."

Zoe knew Mo was right. She remembered Mr Pinch's warning yesterday. But they were too late. Just as Mo finished speaking, an angry voice bellowed down the path, "What on earth. . .? This is the last straw!"

Zoe and Mo turned to see Mr Pinch marching towards them, his face very pink and cross. "Those messy hippos have destroyed their enclosure and they're running wild! They're ruining my lovely

clean zoo!" he snapped. "And now I'm going to have to get this fence mended. Four hippos together in one enclosure are just too many – especially with that naughty little one causing trouble all the time." He jabbed a finger through the air towards Henry.

"But he doesn't mean to cause trouble. He's just playing," Zoe protested, but Mr Pinch cut her off.

"I won't stand for this any longer," he told her and Mo. "I'm going to do something about this – just you wait and see!"

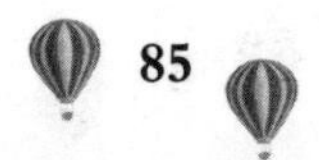

Chapter Six
Mr Pinch's Plan

As Mr Pinch stomped away, muttering angrily to himself, Zoe rushed after him.

"Mr Pinch, wait!" she cried. "What do you mean, you're going to do something? You're not going to send Henry away, are you?"

"Even better – I'm going to send them

all away," snapped Mr Pinch. "I've been speaking to a zoo manager at another zoo, two hundred miles away. They have a hippo enclosure too, with much more space. They're prepared to take all four hippos."

Zoe stared at him. "But – but you can't send them all away," she stuttered. "Albert and Rona have lived here ever since Great-Uncle Horace first opened the zoo. Hetty was born here. And Henry has only just started to settle in!"

"While Mr Higgins is away on his Arctic trip, *I* am in charge of the zoo," Mr Pinch retorted. "That baby might only be small now, but he'll be fully grown before we know it and then he'll cause even more chaos. There just isn't enough room for them all. The hippos have to go."

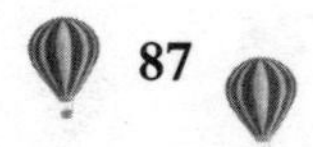

Zoe felt completely helpless. As she watched Mr Pinch storm off, tears sprang to her eyes and rolled down her cheeks. First the news about having to go to Auntie Edna's house, and now this. Things couldn't get any worse!

"What are we going to do, Zoe?"

squeaked Meep. "We can't let Mr Pinch send the hippos away!"

Zoe took a deep breath. "We'll go and talk to Mum. She might be able to speak to Mr Pinch and convince him to let them stay."

"But won't you be late for the last day of school, Zoe?" squeaked Meep anxiously.

"This is far more important!" Zoe told him. "Come on!"

Zoe and Meep ran through the zoo, not even stopping to speak to their animal friends who called out to wish them good morning. They raced to the zoo hospital and burst through the door.

"Mum, Mum!" Zoe gasped breathlessly.

"Goodness, Zoe, what's the matter?" said Lucy, turning round. She was sitting

at her computer, tapping away. "I'm just booking my flights to the Arctic. I need to get it all done today."

"Mum, the hippos broke their fence and Mr Pinch says he's going to send them all to another zoo," explained Zoe quickly. "He thinks they're too big and too messy for their enclosure! Can you talk to him?"

"Oh dear, that's awful," said Lucy, frowning. "Of course I'll talk to him. But, Zoe, Mr Pinch is the zoo manager, and when Great-Uncle Horace is away, he is in charge. I'm not sure I'll be able to change his mind."

"But you *have* to!" said Zoe. "We can't let him send the hippos away – this is their home!"

"I know, love. But Mr Pinch might have a point," Lucy said gently. "That

enclosure was fine when it was just Albert and Rona, but now there's Hetty and Henry too, and it is looking very cramped in there. When Henry is fully grown we'll have four adult hippos living together – and you know how big they are. I don't always agree with everything Mr Pinch says, but he may be right about there not being enough space for them here. Maybe it would be for the best."

There was a little beeping sound from the computer and Lucy turned back to it, distracted. "Oh, Zoe, I need to finish doing this before all the seats on this flight sell out. I'm sorry. We can have another chat about this when you get home from school, OK? You don't want to be late."

Zoe sighed and said goodbye to Meep, then trudged to school, turning everything

over in her mind. It was all going wrong! She felt so upset that she didn't even want to join in with the end-of-term games on the school field that her teacher had arranged for her class.

"Please can I just watch, Miss Hawkins?" she asked quietly.

"Of course, Zoe," Miss Hawkins replied, looking concerned. "Let me know if you want to talk about anything that's worrying you, won't you?"

Zoe nodded and sat at the edge of the field. Her friends Nicola and Jack ran over.

"Zoe, what's wrong? Aren't you going to come and play?" Nicola asked.

"I don't really feel like it," Zoe said. She explained everything that had happened, with her having to go and stay with her

aunt, and the problem with the hippos.

Jack pulled a face when Zoe described what she could remember of Auntie Edna. "She sounds a bit like my Auntie Muriel," he told her. "I wouldn't want to go and stay with her for the summer either!"

"We'll write you lots of emails and postcards, Zoe," Nicola promised.

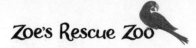

"And I'll ask my mum if we could come and pick you up from your aunt's house one day and take you out somewhere," added Jack.

"Thanks," Zoe told them both gratefully. Her friends had made her feel better, but she was still not looking forward to the holidays at all. And most of all, she was very worried about her hippo friends.

When Zoe got home from school, Meep was waiting for her in his usual spot at the zoo gates, and together they headed straight back to the hippo enclosure.

Mo was mending the broken fence with the help of another zookeeper, Jess, who usually looked after the otters. Mo was holding an armful of wooden boards, and

Jess a hammer and a bag of nails. They both waved when they saw Zoe, but Zoe thought that Mo was looking gloomy.

"Mr Pinch must have told him that he wants to send the hippos away, Meep," Zoe whispered.

She let herself into the enclosure with her special necklace and found Henry rolling around in the mud, looking as happy as ever. The other hippos were snoozing in the sun. It was obvious they hadn't heard the news yet.

"Hi, Henry," whispered Zoe, bending down as he jumped up and trotted over to her. "Listen – Meep and I need to tell you something." Henry snuffled a little, and Zoe continued. "The thing is, Mr Pinch doesn't think there's enough room for all the hippos in this enclosure. He wants to

send you all far away, to a different zoo!"

Zoe waited nervously to see what the little hippo's reaction would be. But even on hearing this news, Henry didn't seem too sad. He put his head on one side, thinking. Then he gave a cheery little snort.

Zoe nodded, smiling in surprise. "That's true, Henry. You have already had lots of fun at the Rescue Zoo, and the new zoo might be just as lovely."

Henry added another little grunt and Zoe smiled. "You're right – at least you'll still be with your new hippo friends. Henry, you're always so cheerful, no matter what! Don't you ever feel sad or worried? You must have had some really difficult times, like when you lost your family, and when you were flown all the way over here to live in a new country?"

Henry thought for a moment, then nodded and gave another little grunt. Zoe smiled at him. "I hadn't thought about it like that before," she told him. "All the sad or scary things that happened to you – they

led to you coming here. So everything worked out for the best in the end. Maybe that's what I need to think about having to go away for the summer, and

about you and the other hippos leaving. Everything will work out for the best." She stroked his head. "It's funny, Henry. Usually I'm the one who helps out an animal at the zoo with a problem, but this time you've helped me!"

Henry nudged Zoe's leg again with his snout and gave a happy little snort, looking very pleased and proud.

"Let's go and see how Mo is getting on with fixing the fence, shall we?" suggested Zoe.

They walked over to where Mo and Jess were just about to fix the last wooden board in place. Henry watched with interest, then gave a playful little squeal and ducked through the gap still in the fence. Zoe giggled as the funny little hippo darted around the patch of grass

and ran around the zookeepers' legs before Mo managed to guide him back into his enclosure again. "There you go, Henry! We've had enough hippos on the loose today," he chuckled.

As Zoe set off for home, waving goodbye to Mo and Henry, she walked past the empty patch of grassland next to the hippos' enclosure that Henry had been scampering around a few moments before – and suddenly her eyes went wide. "Meep! We need to find Mum," she said urgently. "I think I've got an idea. It might mean the hippos can stay at the zoo after all!"

Chapter Seven
Helping the Hippos

"Hold on tight, Meep!" said Zoe, and the little lemur clung to her shoulder with his strong fingers. Zoe started running, and didn't stop until the zoo hospital was in sight. "Mum!" she called as she darted through the door. "Mum, I need to talk to you!"

Lucy was tidying away boxes of different-sized bandages in the store room. "Goodness, Zoe, that's the second time today you've arrived here looking like you've just run a race! Is everything OK? How was your last day at school?"

"Mum, listen – I've had an idea," Zoe explained. "Mr Pinch wants to send the hippos away to another zoo because he says their enclosure isn't big enough for them all, and that's why they're causing so much chaos and mess. But there's a big patch of empty grassland right next to their enclosure! It's not being used for anything at the moment. If we just moved the fence, we could make that area part of the hippos' enclosure too. It would be lots bigger! I'm sure it would be big enough for the hippos to stay!"

Lucy looked surprised. "Zoe, that's such a good idea. I wonder why we've never thought of doing that before!" Then her face fell. "The only problem is, Mr Pinch has already arranged for the hippos to be transported to their new home tomorrow. If we're going to change his mind, we'd need to do it very quickly."

"Let's ask some of the other zookeepers to help!" suggested Zoe. "If there are lots of us working together, we'll be able to move the fence in no time!"

Lucy hesitated, looking a little unsure.

"Please, Mum!" said Zoe. "We can't let Mr Pinch send the hippos away!"

Lucy looked at Zoe, then smiled, switched on her walkie-talkie and spoke into it. "Come in, all zookeepers!" she said. "We need help with an urgent job at

the hippo enclosure. Please meet me and Zoe there in five minutes!"

Zoe grinned happily. By the time she and her mum arrived at the hippo enclosure there was a crowd of keepers gathering, with more arriving all the time. Zoe was thrilled to see them all waiting, eager to find out what was going on – especially Mo. Lucy quickly explained Zoe's plan and there was a buzz of excited chatter.

"That's a perfect idea. I've always thought that empty patch of grass was just wasted space!" Zoe heard Bill, the crocodile keeper, say.

"I'll fetch the tools we used to fix the fence earlier on!" said Mo, rushing off, while another group ran to find some more wooden planks to use to make the

fence longer, and Lucy went to collect a tray of cold drinks for everyone.

During all the commotion, Zoe managed to speak to the hippos.

"We've got an idea that might mean you can all stay at the zoo," she whispered to them, and smiled as their dark eyes lit up. "But it's really, really important that you all behave while we're working on it, OK? If there's any mud or mess, or if the fence gets broken again, then Mr Pinch might still say you've got to leave." She smiled at Henry and added, "Especially you, Henry. Do you think you can do that for me?"

Albert, Rona and Hetty all nodded their huge grey heads, while Henry gave an excited grunt, promising to be good too. Zoe rushed back towards the crowd of zookeepers.

"Can I help?" she called to Mo, eager to be involved. "What can I do?"

Mo thought for a moment. "Why don't you keep an eye on cheeky little Henry? We're going to have to pull the fence down so that we can move it, and I don't want him to escape, especially if Mr Pinch is doing one of his rounds!"

"Sure, I'll keep an eye on him – but I have a feeling he'll behave!" Zoe told him, grinning to herself.

Three hours later, everyone stood back to take a look at their handiwork. Zoe couldn't believe how different the enclosure looked. Beyond the mud bath, where the fence used to be, there was now a big, flat, grassy patch, covered in daisies. The fence had been moved to the very

far end of the grass area. As soon as it was finished, Zoe whispered to Henry, giving him permission, and the little hippo eagerly ran straight into the new area and trotted all the way around it, grunting eagerly.

"It's nearly twice as big!" Zoe heard one of the keepers comment. "The hippos have got so much more space now!"

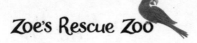

"There's so much extra room, we could even make the mud bath bigger!" Mo said to Lucy. "Twice as big, in fact! I bet the hippos would love that!"

Mr Pinch had turned up just as the final wooden post had been hammered into place. At first he had complained loudly about no one asking his permission to do the work, but Lucy had calmly explained to him that they knew how busy he was, and didn't want to bother him with yet another job. "But you must admit that we've solved the problem!" she added, winking at Zoe. "This enclosure is more than big enough for four hippos. Now there's no reason to send them away. Zoe's idea worked perfectly!"

Mr Pinch glared at Zoe. "I should have known this was your doing," he muttered.

Meep, who was sitting on Zoe's shoulder, stuck his tiny tongue out at Mr Pinch, and the zoo manager spluttered angrily. "That lemur is the cheekiest animal I have ever met," he snapped, his face pink. "While you're away from the zoo for the school holidays, young lady, *he* will be in a cage where he belongs."

With that he marched off, grumbling again. Zoe hugged Meep tightly. She should have known that Mr Pinch would spoil everything! She had been so pleased about the hippos, and horrid Mr Pinch had just reminded her about her other problem: a summer away from the Rescue Zoo.

"It's OK, Meep," she whispered. "Just think positive, like Henry would! Maybe something good will come out of you having to live with the other lemurs and monkeys while I'm away. You might make some really good new friends."

Meep didn't look very sure. "I'll try my best, Zoe," he began – but then he stopped, his ears pricking up. "Zoe!" he squeaked. "It's that noise again. The Rescue Zoo bus!"

Zoe listened and heard the familiar rumble in the distance. She looked at Meep, her eyes wide. "But it can't be, Meep. Great-Uncle Horace set off for the Arctic yesterday morning! He can't be back already . . . can he?"

Chapter Eight
Happy Holidays!

As Zoe and Meep rushed to the zoo gates, she saw that it was definitely Great-Uncle Horace's yellow bus rumbling into the zoo! Great-Uncle Horace honked the horn cheerfully when he saw them, and poked his head through the window.

"Ah, Zoe! I'm back! And you're just the

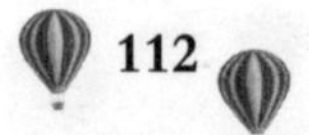

person I wanted to see!"

He parked the bus and jumped out, with Kiki fluttering out after him.

"I don't understand," Zoe said, running up to give him a hug. "You only just left for the research project. Aren't you supposed to be there for six whole weeks?"

Great-Uncle Horace smiled and nodded. "There was a change of plan, my dear. Ah, here's your mum now. Lucy, would you like to tell Zoe the news?"

Zoe looked at her mum nervously. She wasn't sure she wanted more news, after the last time! But Lucy was beaming.

"Zoe, you're not going to have to go to Auntie Edna's after all," she explained, and Zoe felt her heart leap. "When I rang Great-Uncle Horace to tell him that I had decided to join the trip but that it

meant you would have to leave the zoo for the summer, Great-Uncle Horace decided straight away that he didn't want to go."

Zoe stared at Great-Uncle Horace. "But won't you be sad to miss it?" she asked.

Great-Uncle Horace beamed. "Zoe, I've travelled all around the world. I've visited the Arctic lots of times. But do you know something? I realised I would much rather spend the summer *here*, with my favourite great-niece! I'm happy to come back to the Rescue Zoo. And when your mum explained what was happening with the hippos, that was even more reason to come straight home," he added, looking serious. "I'd better go and have a little talk with Percy Pinch. He might be in charge of the zoo while I'm away, but no one sends Rescue Zoo animals away – ever! When an animal comes to the Rescue Zoo, they have a home here for life. Although we do need to work out what to do about the hippos' enclosure, if it's not big enough. . ."

"You don't need to worry about that, Great-Uncle Horace!" Zoe said. "I had an idea! Do you remember the patch of empty grass that was next to the hippo enclosure? Well, Mo and all the other zookeepers helped us to move the fence, so that the grassland is part of the enclosure now. It's made the hippos' home much bigger! It looks brilliant," she added proudly.

Great-Uncle Horace beamed. "Wonderful!" he exclaimed. "That was very quick thinking! Thank you, Zoe. I

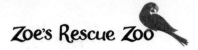

can't wait to see it. In fact, why don't we go there now, so you can show me?"

They all set off for the hippo enclosure together and Zoe found she couldn't help skipping along, she was so excited about how things had turned out. "So . . . I'm really staying here for the summer?" she asked. She almost couldn't believe it.

The Happy Hippo

Suddenly her head was racing with ideas. "I'm going to see Henry and the other hippos every single day. And I'm desperate to play with Gertie's baby. And now that Ruby the macaw's poorly wing is properly healed, I'll go and watch her practise her flying. And—"

Great-Uncle Horace chuckled. "You're going to be very busy, my dear!"

When they reached the lovely new hippo enclosure, Henry rushed straight over to greet them. He thought Zoe must be coming to say goodbye for the summer, but when Great-Uncle Horace and Lucy went off to inspect the new fencing and discuss making the mud bath and pool bigger, Zoe managed to whisper her good news to the little hippo.

"Henry, I don't have to go away for the

holidays after all! There's been a change of plan!" she explained, and giggled as Henry's tail wagged excitedly.

Great-Uncle Horace was astonished at how much bigger the space now was. "This is fantastic!" he exclaimed, walking around and spreading his arms out wide. "Zoe, your clever idea has transformed the hippos' home!"

Meep jumped into Zoe's arms for a hug. "Zoe, I'm so happy that we'll both get to spend the holidays together," he squeaked. "And I'm happy that the hippos won't have to go away. And I'm *very* happy that Mr Pinch didn't get his own way," he added mischievously.

"I'm happy too, Meep," said Zoe, smiling. "The Rescue Zoo feels like an especially happy place, now that Henry

lives here. He was right – things have all worked out for the best in the end!"

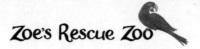

"I'm glad Henry came to live here as well," chattered Meep eagerly. "I wonder what the next new animal to come to the Rescue Zoo will be?"

"I'm not sure, Meep," said Zoe, cuddling her little friend. "But whatever it is, I can't wait to find out!"

Look out for more amazing animal adventures at the Rescue Zoo!

The Rescue Princesses

Have you read them all?

nosy crow